Out of the darkness came the Great Raven, who brought the Sun to the children of the North Pacific Coast.

LORD OF THE SKY

LINDA ZEMAN-SPALENY

illustrated by LUDMILA ZEMAN

TUNDRA BOOKS

Published in Canada by Tundra Books,
75 Sherbourne Street, Toronto, Ontario M5A 2P9

Published in the United States by Tundra Books of Northern
New York,
P.O. Box 1030, Plattsburgh, New York 12901

Library of Congress Control Number: 2008903012

Library and Archives Canada Cataloguing in Publication

Zeman-Spaleny, Linda
        Lord of the sky / author, Linda Zeman-Spaleny ;
Illustrator, Ludmila Zeman.
Based on an animated short film of the same name.
ISBN 978-0-88776-896-5 (bound)

        1. Indians of North America – Folklore – Juvenile literature.
2. Human ecology – Folklore – Juvenile literature. 3. Environmental
protection – Folklore – Juvenile literature. 4. Ravens – Folklore –
Juvenile literature. I. Zeman, Ludmila II. Title. III. Title: Lord of the
sky [videorecording].

E98.F6Z44 2009   j398.2'08997   C2008-902063-4

We acknowledge the financial support of the Government of Canada
through the Book Publishing Industry Development Program (BPIDP)
and that of the Government of Ontario through the Ontario Media
Development Corporation's Ontario Book Initiative.
We further acknowledge the support of the Canada Council for the
Arts and the Ontario Arts Council for our publishing program.

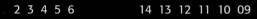 ONTARIO ARTS COUNCIL
CONSEIL DES ARTS DE L'ONTARIO

Medium: pencil, colored pencil, and watercolor on paper

Printed in China

 2 3 4 5 6   14 13 12 11 10 09

To Helena

I remember seeing totem poles for the first time in British Columbia. We had just arrived from Europe. "These glorious carved columns tell stories in wooden pictures," my mom explained. "They were made by the first people of this land."

My parents wanted all the children of the world to know about these wooden picture books from Canada. So, they made a film called *Lord of the Sky*.

Now I am a mom and this is the way I tell the story to my little girl.

Linda

In a village by the sea, there once lived a young boy. Each morning, he would look to the sky and wave to the passing ravens. The warmth of the sun would caress his cheeks as he heard the birds calling. "They are happy in this place," he would say, "as am I. It is their home, and mine." Some days he would say the same of the trees, or the fish, or the waves, or the rain.

All admired the ravens, especially the boy. He would often share leftover food with them. But the birds were not always kind. Some were spoiled and greedy. They squabbled with each other and sometimes even chased children into the woods.

The boy did not mind. He liked their cunning and their confidence. He loved the strong and certain strokes of their shiny black wings. *If only he could fly with them!*
One day, some village boys decided to teach the birds a lesson.

Hiding at the edge of the forest, they watched the ravens steal from the fishermen's catch. The boys threw handfuls of stones. When none found its target, the game turned serious. "No!" cried the boy. "Stop!" But it was too late.

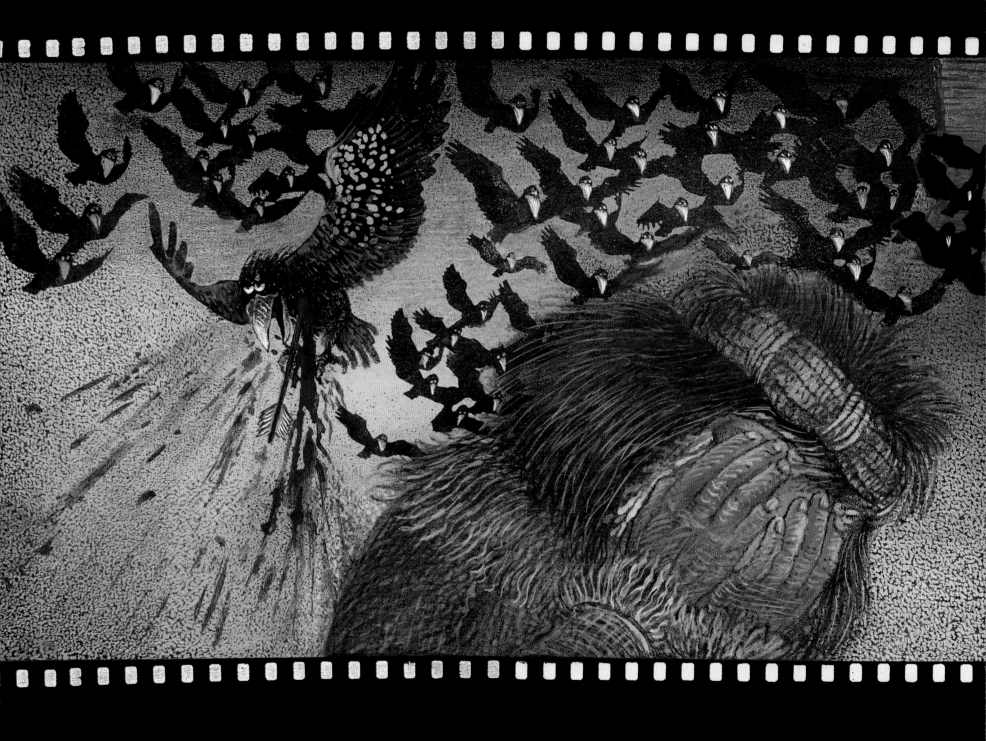

A swift arrow with a sharp edge led to a fatal end.

Shrieking squawks replaced the deadly silence, and rustling black wings filled the sky.
Darkness crept over the land.

"What have you done?" asked the wise elder. "The raven is our brother. Without sun, there can be no life!" The wise elder then looked at the men of the village. "Lord of the Sky. He alone can help us. Go to him."

All the men lowered their heads. No one moved.

Only the boy slipped quietly away. Never to see the sun again, never to feel its warmth was too much to bear. He would go for help. He pushed a canoe onto the sea.

Hour after hour he paddled, further and further from all that he knew. His arms ached. Seawater stung his eyes, and his empty stomach churned. When the sea turned calm, he was asleep in an instant.

While the boy slept, the waves rose up like giant sea monsters. They lifted the boat and tossed it onto the rocky shore. At last all was calm, but the boy kept his eyes closed. *This dream will end soon*, he thought. Then he heard gentle chirping.

The boy scrambled onto a stone ledge. "Come, little one. Don't be frightened." At first the bird was hesitant, but the boy won its trust. His eyes searched the cliffs. High up in the clouds, a giant nest crowned a rocky tower.

The boy began to climb, always looking above, not ever below. He felt stones crumble beneath his feet, but never heard them hit the ground. Stiff with fear, he pushed on, knowing that he must help the little bird. As he lowered it to safety, a horrendous rolling rumble descended from above.

A powerful gust sent the boy crashing to the edge of the nest as an enormous bird
landed. He shivered, unable to utter a word.

"I know what you foolish humans have done," snarled the bird. It looked at its
young. "But you are brave and kind, so I will help you." The giant bird lowered its head,
and the boy climbed onto its back.

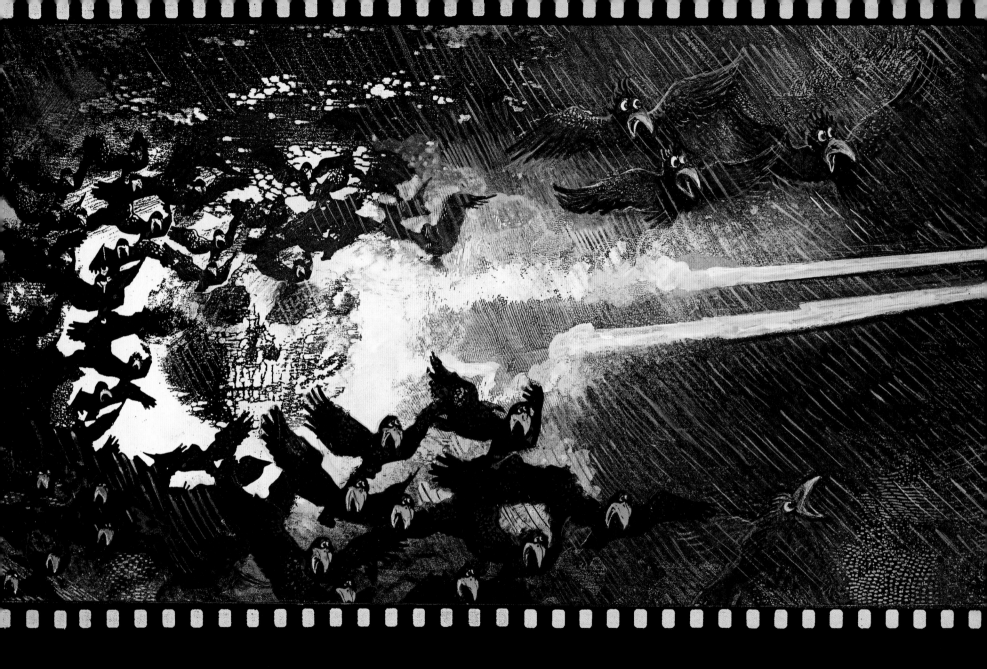

A few flaps of huge wings sent the two hurtling across the sky. The boy pressed his body flat against the bird to keep from sliding off and dropping out of the clouds.

From beneath the beating wings, thunder roared and the sky exploded with rain. "Thunderbird!" the boy exclaimed. Lightning blasted from its eyes and ripped through the sky, scattering the ravens in all directions.

The winds howled and beat against the boy's chest. "There's my village," cried the boy. "There's my home!" Never had he imagined what it would feel like to soar so high above the earth.

Tightly he clasped the thunderbird's feathers. His heart pounded as he saw golden rays of sunlight dancing on the waves and felt warmth upon his skin once again.

"Thunderbird!" cried the children on the shore. "Lord of the Sky!" The bird's mighty talons touched down amidst a storm of swirling sand. To everyone's surprise, the boy slid down off its back.

The boy stood as a hero, his hand upon the great thunderbird. He had found a way
to return light and life to the village. He could be happy in his home once again.

This is a story of things that happened in the past. But it is still true today that to remain in light, our home, our world, must be cared for.